FRED
AND THE PET SHOW PANIC

The Adventures of Fred
Published by Fawcett Columbine

FRED
AND THE PET SHOW PANIC

by Leslie McGuire

Illustrated by Dave Henderson

Fawcett Columbine • New York

A Fawcett Columbine Book
Published by Ballantine Books

Copyright © 1991 by Mega-Books of New York, Inc.

Library of Congress Catalog Card Number:
90-83160
ISBN: 0-449-90503-9

Design by Holly Johnson

Manufactured in the United States of America

First Edition: April 1991
10 9 8 7 6 5 4 3 2 1

CONTENTS

CHAPTER ONE

THERE'S ONLY ONE BEST PET

Monday evening started out nice and quiet. But the peace didn't last very long. Arnie and Beth and Mike were watching television. Katie was up in her room listening to that awful noise she calls music.

Then Mr. Duff came home and made everyone change the TV channel. That was the beginning of the disaster. Not that I am against changing the channel, you understand. The show the kids were watching was not educational. It was a silly cartoon. I think they should have been reading books. Reading would be much better for those children. I know. I read all the time.

By the way, I'm Fred. I am the Duff family

dog. I am a Saint Bernard. We are those dogs who save you when you get lost in a snowstorm, or stuck in a mud slide. We carry little barrels of brandy under our chins. We are supposed to give the brandy to the people we rescue.

I think brandy is a silly thing to give people. It tastes terrible. Chicken soup would be better. But no one ever asks me what I think. They should. I may be a dog, but I know an awful lot about what is good for humans.

Anyway, the Duffs live in a little town called Big Bluff. The town is called Big Bluff because there is a big cliff that goes right down to the harbor. The Duffs have a house on top of the cliff. They like to call it Duff's Bluff. They like their house and their cliff a lot.

I like the house. But I hate the cliff. Someone is always getting too close to the edge of the cliff. And I have to make sure they don't get hurt. If the Duffs were more careful, I wouldn't worry about them. But they never think about what they are doing. Especially Mr. Duff. He is very careless. Mr. Duff likes to mow the lawn every weekend. Every weekend I have to save him from falling off the cliff. But does he thank me? No. Every weekend he calls me a fathead.

Mrs. Duff is the most careful person in the family. She doesn't need too much rescuing. I am glad about that, because the rest of the family needs a lot of rescuing. Katie Duff is a teenager. For some reason, she can't cross streets without help. She never looks at the light. And she never looks both ways. I always have to throw myself in front of her so she won't get hit by a car. She gets very cranky about this. But I don't mind. Safe is safe, I always say.

Arnie Duff is the biggest problem. Arnie is little. I am taller than Arnie when I am sitting down and he is standing up. But smallness isn't the big problem. His problem is that he never looks where he is going. It's not that he can't see. Arnie can see just fine. Last summer he got glasses. Before that, he couldn't see anything. Now he can see everything.

Arnie always races off to get a better look at something silly, like a fly, or a motorcycle. I spend most of my time rescuing Arnie from whatever is between him and the thing he wants to get a look at. I also have to save Beth and Mike.

Beth Woods and Mike Peese are Arnie's best friends. Beth's father is a scientist. He collects things like spiders and snakes and frogs. So does Beth. She says she's rescuing them. From what, I ask? Spiders and snakes and frogs don't need rescuing. They are fine right where they are—wherever that is. But at least her heart is in the right place.

Mike likes to take pictures of things. He always carries a camera. This is good, because he gets great shots of me rescuing the Duffs. For some reason, the Duffs don't like the pictures. Especially Katie Duff. I guess teenagers don't like getting their picture taken. I'm sure she will get over that one day.

Anyway, where was I? Oh, yes. Mr. Duff made the kids change the channel. He wanted to watch the news. Usually the kids won't watch the news. And this time it would have been better if they hadn't.

The news had a story about a big pet show that was held in the city. The TV flashed on a picture of all these dogs and cats with bows in their hair. The animals had pushed-in faces and silly ways of walking. I tried very hard not to laugh.

The kids, however, got very excited. They started talking about what kind of pet was the best to have. It was a ridiculous discussion. Obviously, a Saint Bernard is the best kind of pet to have.

Katie said that cats were good because they caught mice. Mike said horses were good because you could ride them. Beth said sheep were good because they gave wool. Beth also said caterpillars were good because they made silk. But Beth is not your average kid.

But they were wrong. A pet who saves your life is the best kind of pet to have. In other words, a pet like me.

Then Beth said every pet has something very good to offer their humans. Take her pet frog, Mary Lou, for example. She said Mary Lou was her best friend. I think Mary Lou is a bore. But she's not *my* pet frog, so I decided not to bring that up. That's when Beth said it was silly to say one pet was the best of all.

I'm happy to report that here Arnie started to stick up for me. Arnie can be counted on to take my side. I like him even more for that. Arnie said I was the best pet in the world. He's correct, of course. But right after that, Arnie messed up.

First, Katie said that all kids think *their* pet is the best one. That's when Arnie said the kids should hold a pet show in Big Bluff— right in the front yard of the Duffs' house! Aaargh!

CHAPTER TWO

RED IS NOT A DOG COLOR

A pet show in the front yard? It was an awful idea. But no one else seemed to think so. First Beth, then Katie, then Mike, and finally Arnie, started to come up with dumb ideas for this pet show. Soon they had a plan. It could only mean disaster.

I went outside. I could not stand to listen for another second. Winston was outside.

Winston is a dog. But he is not a Saint Bernard. He is a pug. Pugs have squashed-in noses. Winston looks as if he ran into a door at full speed. And when he talks, he sounds like a clogged drain.

Winston was talking with Sam and Janet.

Sam and Janet are two Siamese cats that live on the other side of Winston's house.

I told Winston the awful news.

"What's wrong with a pet show?" Winston asked. "I bet I'll win first prize!"

That made me laugh. How could Winston win first prize? After all, I, Fred, the Great Houdini of Dogs, the Savior of the Duffs (and others), would naturally be in the pet show. Therefore, it should be obvious who was going to win first prize. Me, right?

That is when I realized that it was silly of me to object to this pet show. After all, since I was going to win first prize and a blue ribbon, what could go wrong?

I felt a lot better. I thanked Winston and went back inside the house. By this time, Beth and Mike had gone home. The Duffs were eating dinner. They were all talking about the pet show.

"How sweet!" said Mrs. Duff.

"Very democratic," said Mr. Duff.

"Yes," said Katie. "That way, no one will feel bad."

9

"We'll have a prize for each pet," said Arnie. "Instead of a blue ribbon for the best pet, we're going to give *everyone* a prize."

Everyone? A prize for what? I thought. That's the craziest idea I ever heard. But Arnie went on.

"We'll give prizes for the longest nose, or the most beautiful fur," Arnie said.

Totally dim-witted. But I decided that maybe I could convince them to give a special prize. What is wrong with Best in Show? They could give the other prizes, too.

I quickly left the dining room. I raced into the hall. Good. The pile of newspapers was still sitting there. Mr. Duff hadn't put them out yet. I knocked them over and started looking for an article about the pet show in the city. After all, those people are smart. They give Best in Show to the best pet, don't they? Why can't the kids?

I found a few articles. I tore out the parts about Best in Show. I left one on the coffee table. I left one on Arnie's bed. I figured they would get the idea after a while. I mean, how dumb could they be?

That was my first mistake.

Well, the kids spent the rest of the week making prize ribbons, painting signs, and getting the yard ready for the big day. I, of course, had to watch them every minute. They put the signs up all over town. They stuck them on trees, on lampposts, in the library, on bulletin boards, outside the supermarket—phew!

By Friday morning, I was tired. But I had no time to rest. I still had a few things I needed to take care of.

Arnie was in the garage painting a banner. In case you don't know what a banner is, it's a very, very long sign. The banner said: DUFFS' PET SHOW TODAY. Arnie was planning to string it up between the two oak trees in the front yard. Arnie had a big jar of red paint on the worktable in the garage. I, of course, had to sit in the garage with him. The garage is a dangerous place. There are saws and hammers and cans of gasoline all over the place. Arnie is clumsy sometimes. He could get hurt.

I was lying under the worktable with one eye open. I always keep one eye open around Arnie. You never know what he'll do next. Anyway, I was waiting for Arnie to get finished painting. Then suddenly Fudge showed up.

Did I forget to tell you about Fudge? Probably. Personally, I would rather forget about Fudge altogether.

Fudge is a cat. He is young. He is a pain in the neck. Among his most annoying habits is the fact that he always calls me Mom. I hate that. Fudge is black and white, and a trouble-maker.

The kids found Fudge in the old Griswold mansion. But that's another story. They named him Vanilla Fudge because he is black with a white stripe. That is a sickeningly cute name. They call him Fudge for short. I do not think he is cute.

Fudge has been taking cat lessons from Sam and Janet. He spends most of his time doing pouncing practice. Mostly, he pounces on me. I hate that, too.

Anyway, Fudge came sneaking into the garage. Without any warning at all, he took a flying leap from a cardboard box. He landed on the table. That was better than landing on me. But not much. He skidded across the tabletop and knocked over the jar of red paint. The paint spilled all over the table. Then it poured down all over my head!

Arnie got mad. But I got madder. Red is not a dog color. We chased Fudge back outside. Then Arnie got some paper towels and tried to clean up. He tried to wipe the table. But he just made it worse. He smeared paint all over the place. He also wiped my head. Naturally, he got paint all over the rest of me.

Clearly I was going to have to clean myself up. I decided to head down to the salt marsh.

I could get wet in the shallow water, then roll in the sand. That usually takes care of messes. But I never made it to the marsh.

I was on my way across the yard when suddenly Mrs. Duff called me.

I thought perhaps she had a small snack for me. I forgot about the red paint. I raced into the kitchen. But a snack was not what she had in mind. It was a bath!

I hate baths.

The next thing I knew, she had me outside, covered in soap bubbles. Then she turned the hose on me!

CHAPTER THREE

ARRESTED!

I was scrubbed. I was rubbed. I was dried with a towel. I was blown to bits with a blow dryer. Aargh!

But I tried to look on the bright side. After all, at least I would be clean and fluffy for the pet show. I should definitely look my best. After all, I was going to win Best in Show. The bath was worth it.

Finally I was dry. But I still had a lot of things to do. The most important thing was to head down to the newspaper office. I decided this was probably a great chance to get on the front page of the *Big Bluff News.* But first I needed a photograph of myself.

I headed for Arnie's room. I pushed the

box of pictures out from under his bed. I emptied them on the floor and looked until I found a good one. A great one, actually. It was a shot of the time I saved Arnie from falling off the end of the slide in the park. I had him by the shirt collar. I looked very strong in that picture.

I took a few other pictures, too. Mike always gets great shots of me during my rescues. He has his camera hanging around his neck instead of a barrel of brandy. He's sort of a Saint Bernard of photographers. I still don't understand why the Duffs get annoyed when he takes pictures of them being rescued. I suppose it's because they don't always look too good in the pictures.

Anyway, I had to take the pictures and one of the flyers to the newspaper office. I planned to leave them on the doorstep of the newspaper office. This was a problem. I would have to carry them in my mouth. That meant a few teeth marks. But there was nothing I could do about that. The newspaper was going to need all the material it could get. They would probably send a reporter and a photographer to the Duffs' pet show. They needed those rescue shots. I knew they would want to have a lot of pictures of me when I won Best in Show.

I went down to Main Street. I put the pictures and the flyers on the steps of the newspaper office. Then I barked about sixty times. That usually brings someone to the door. For some dumb reason, nobody came.

I decided to howl. If barking doesn't get someone to come, howling usually works. I sat down on the step and stuck my nose in the air. I howled my best howl. Still, nobody came to the door.

Actually, I was starting to like the sound of the howl. Maybe I should sing a song, I thought. After all, what could be more exciting to a newspaper than a prize rescue dog who can sing? I decided I would howl "Rudolph the Red-Nosed Reindeer."

Just then I heard noises. Someone was coming to the door! I knew it! They just can't stay away from a great singer. I gave the pictures and the flyer a shove with my foot and waited. The door opened, and suddenly a hand grabbed the fur on the back of my neck!

I looked up. A man wearing a gray suit and a pair of black glasses was holding me by the fur.

"What's the matter, boy?" the man asked. "Are you lost?"

There was nothing the matter with me. So what was the matter with him anyway? Did I look lost? No.

I gave the pictures and the flyer another push with my foot. Of course, all he had to do was pick them up. Then he would know right away that he was dealing with a star. But did he do that? No.

"You don't look like you've been lost for long," said the newspaper man, smiling. But he didn't let go of me, either. "You look like you have been getting fed pretty well lately."

What did he know? I had not gotten even one snack today.

20

"Well, let's have a look at your tag," he said. "We'll make sure you get home safe. We'll also tell your family what you've been up to. Perhaps you shouldn't be allowed to run all over town, boy."

The nerve, I thought, as he messed around with my neck fur. He was trying to find my collar. This town would be a lot worse off without a rescue dog like myself! But then again, this man probably did not know the first thing about safety!

"Well, boy," he finally said, "it looks like you don't have a collar. Maybe you *are* lost!"

What? No collar? Of course I had a collar. And a very nice one, too, I might add. Was this man blind?

Then suddenly I remembered something awful. I had just had a bath. I knew I felt sort of funny. But I thought I felt funny from being fluffed and rubbed and blown to bits. I was wrong. Something was missing.

I felt funny because Mrs. Duff had forgotten to put my collar back on!

CHAPTER FOUR

THE DOGGY BIG HOUSE

Well, what happened next was so terrible, I still have trouble talking about it.

The newspaperman got a rope and tied it around my neck. Then he went inside and called the pound. He never even saw the pictures!

Next thing I knew, I was headed for jail. The doggy big house. The slammer.

The truck from the pound was lined with cages. Now, I am a big dog. But the guy from the pound had a big stick. And there was a round rope on the end of it. I think you call that rope a noose. He slipped the noose over my head. Then he tightened it. Next he pushed me into the truck. One of the cages was opened. He pushed me inside and shut the door. Then he slid the noose off my head.

He slammed the back door, and off we went. The ride in that truck was not smooth. These people should really take better care of their trucks.

Next thing I knew, I was being unloaded into an even bigger cage at the pound. And I wasn't the only animal in the place, either.

There were all kinds of things there. Dogs, cats, and even a big snake! And talk about gloomy! This was not the happiest place on the planet, let me tell you.

At first, all I could do was sit in the corner of my cage and feel sorry for myself.

After all, it was Friday. The pet show was Saturday. How was I supposed to win Best in Show if I was locked up in jail? I had to get out of this place. But how?

I went over everything.

The Duffs could come and get me. But they could only do that if they knew where I was. They didn't know I was in jail. They wouldn't even figure out that I was missing for a few more hours!

I could escape. But how? The cage was tall. Too tall to jump. Besides, the cage had a top. True. The door was locked. I am the Great Houdini of Dogs. But there were no windows. There was nothing to stand on. I didn't have a key to the door. Even if I did, the lock was on the outside. Besides, I don't have fingers.

Maybe they let the dogs out for a run, I thought. Maybe there was a way of escaping then. I needed more facts. I decided I had to question one of these dogs.

I lifted my head. In the next cage there was a very sorry example of a dog. He looked like a cross between a collie and a poodle. An interesting mix. He was not beautiful. His head was big, but his nose was pointy. His fur was crinkly and matted. It was a bunch of strange colors. There was gray, white (sort of), black, and tan. This was mixed with mud and what looked like axle

grease. This dog would not win Best in Show.

"Excuse me," I said.

The dog looked up.

"My name is Fred," I said. "I'm in here by mistake."

"Aren't we all," said the dog. "My name is Butch."

"So, Butch," I said. "What are the chances of breaking out of this place?"

"None," said Butch. Then he put his head back down. It was not a good sign.

"Er, how long have you been in here?" I asked.

"Three weeks," he said.

Yikes, I thought. That's *way* too long. But I didn't give up. After all, Butch might not be too smart. He might not have had a good escape plan.

"That's too long," I said. "Tell me what goes on in this place."

"Not much," said Butch. "They lock up and go home at five-thirty in the afternoon. Right before that, they feed us, and change our water. In the morning, they come back at eight o'clock. They hose down the cages."

"That's it?" I asked. "No walks, no nothing?"

"No nothing," said Butch. "But the food isn't bad."

This was not good. There was a big, round clock on the wall. The clock said four-thirty. If the Duffs didn't show up to rescue me within the next hour, I was sunk.

I sat down. I needed to think. Now, when I think, I like to chew on magazines. That's why I read so much. I read a lot of interesting articles while I'm chewing. But there was nothing to read.

I decided to chew on my foot.

That's when I noticed a piece of paper stuck to my fur. I pulled it off. I probably picked it up outside the newspaper office. I dropped it on the floor. I chewed on my foot and stared at the lock on the door.

I thought, and I chewed. Nothing came to me.

Then I heard a lot of clanging and banging. A teenager came into the cellblock. He was the keeper. He had a big bag of dog chow. He opened each cage. Then he poured dog food into the bowl in the cage. It didn't smell good to me. But then, I was used to Mrs. Duff's cooking.

I watched as the keeper added water to each water bowl in the cage. After he finished, he would go back out and shut the cage door. It locked automatically.

And that's when I had the idea!

I wasn't the Great Houdini of Dogs for nothing!

CHAPTER FIVE

THE PERFECT ESCAPE

First thing I did was find that piece of paper that had been stuck in my fur. I popped it in my mouth. I started chewing. As I chewed, I watched the keeper come closer and closer to my cage door.

Finally I had the paper chewed into a nice, soft, sticky little wad. And just in time, too.

I stood right next to the door. The kid opened the door.

"Hello there, boy," he said. Then he patted me on the head.

I didn't make a move. The kid walked inside. He bent over and filled the food bowl. While his head was down, I stretched my neck. I angled my mouth right to where the latch on the door was. I pushed the wad of paper into the little hole. That was the catch in the lock. I pushed hard with my tongue so it wouldn't fall out.

The keeper didn't notice. Phew.

He filled my water bowl. Then he stood up and slammed the door. I listened for the little click that tells you when the latch has caught. There was no little click. He wouldn't have heard it anyway. First of all, the dogs and cats were all munching and slurping. Someone should give these guys a lecture on eating habits and manners someday. Second of all, humans don't have very good ears.

At five-thirty on the dot, the keeper came back. He checked us. Then he turned out the light. I heard the doors shut behind him.

I decided to wait a bit and see what happened. It was still light out. I figured that I'd better wait until dark. I didn't want to get caught sneaking out. Hopefully my wad of paper would stay put.

I waited until six-thirty. Then I tested the

door. I put my paw under the first bar and pushed hard. It opened!

Butch sat right up, and so did the other dogs and cats.

"Hey," said Butch. "How'd you do that?"

"Simple," I said. Then I explained about the wad of paper. "Next time the keeper comes through here with the food bag, just tear a little piece off."

"Thanks, buddy," said Butch with a grin. "Good luck!"

I nodded and went out of the kennels. There was an open window at the back of the office. I stood on my hind legs and shoved hard with my head. The window opened enough for me to squeeze through. In a second I was free! The air smelled good. It felt good. Brains and luck were on my side. I was very glad I hadn't lost my touch. Then I raced down the street and headed for home!

By the time I got in the door, it was after seven. The Duffs had already finished eating.

31

"Well, my goodness, Fred," said Mrs. Duff. "Where have *you* been?"

I didn't bother explaining. I checked to see what was on the table first. One of the great things about Mrs. Duff is that she forgets things. This wasn't too good in the case of my collar. But the part I like is that she forgets to put food away. I always check the table. Whenever she leaves something out, I eat it.

I eat it to protect the family, of course. Anyone with any sense knows that if you leave food out, it goes bad. I wouldn't want anyone to get sick, now would I? Of course not. I eat the food to keep my family from getting sick. I am a very noble dog.

Just then Arnie came racing into the kitchen.

"Hey, Fred, we were worried about you!" he said.

They should have been worried. They should have noticed that I am *never* late for dinner. If I am late for dinner, it is either because I have been run over by a truck or I

32

am locked in jail. But do they think of these things? No. Oh well. I guess it's silly of me to expect a lot from humans. After all, they are not Saint Bernards. What do they know about rescues?

Then I noticed that half the food in my bowl was gone.

That awful Fudge ate my food! Fudge loves my food. He loves my bowl. When he was a kitten, he used to curl up and go to sleep in my bowl. I did not like that. But eating my food is worse.

I decided to go outside and find him. I would show that sneaky cat a thing or two.

Winston was sitting in the yard.

"Where were you?" he said.

I told him everything that happened. He was very impressed. He really liked the part about the wadded-up paper.

"How did you ever think of something so smart?" he asked.

"I am just naturally smart," I said.

That's when I heard Sam and Janet, the cats who live next door, start to sing. At least,

that's what Sam and Janet call it. I think their singing sounds like broken violins. It is not a good sound. Then I heard another voice in there too. Fudge.

More cat lessons. Now it was singing practice. Aaaargh.

I suddenly remembered my mission.

CHAPTER SIX

THE THIRD AND WORST MISTAKE

"Gotta go," I said.

"What's the problem?" asked Winston.

"That dumb Fudge ate half my dinner again," I said.

"Maybe he's not as dumb as you think," said Winston. "Which reminds me. How are the reading lessons going?"

"Not well," I said.

"Why?" asked Winston. "Fudge can't learn his alphabet?"

"No," I said. It was depressing me just to think about it. "He's already reading *Cosmopolitan.*"

"That's pretty good," said Winston.

"Why did you say the reading lessons weren't going well?"

"I said that because the only thing worse than a dumb cat is a smart cat," I replied. "He's started giving me advice."

"What's wrong with that?" asked Winston.

"He's a troublemaker," I answered. "Troublemakers do not give good advice."

Winston started to laugh. When Winston talks, he sounds like a clogged drain. But when Winston laughs, he makes a terrible noise. He sounds like a very small garbage truck grinding up a full load of garbage. Personally I didn't see anything funny about Fudge being able to read. But sometimes Winston has a strange sense of humor.

"You are jealous," said Winston when he was finished grinding—or laughing.

"I certainly am not," I said. But I was angry. "Excuse me. I have something to do."

I went around to the side fence. Sam and Janet and Fudge were sitting on the fence singing. That was usually where they sat

when they sang. Fudge does not need singing lessons. I wish those two would leave
Fudge alone. They say they *have* to give him
cat lessons. They are afraid he will start to
think like a dog. But what would be so bad
about that, I say? Every cat on the planet
would be better off thinking like a dog.

So I watched them sing for a while. Then
I went back around the side of the house. I
hid in a bush. I decided to give Fudge a taste
of his own medicine.

I would wait until they finished singing.
Fudge had to come this way to get back in
the house. I had a little surprise planned.

The singing stopped. I waited. Soon I
heard the pitter-patter of little cat feet. I
peeked out from my bush. Sure enough, a
small black animal with a white stripe across
its nose and down its back was walking along
the stone path.

Look out, Fudge, I thought. Because now
I'm going to pay you back for insulting me.
I'm going to pay you back for doing pounc-
ing practice on me. I'm going to pay you

back for all the food you stole from my bowl!
And not only that, you will pay for calling
me Mom all the time.

I leapt out from behind the bush and
landed with all four feet on either side of

39

Fudge. Fudge flattened himself on the ground for a second. Then he did a very weird thing.

Fudge did a handstand.

That's when I discovered that I had just made my third mistake. And it was the worst one yet. This was definitely not my week.

I smelled a terrible smell. It was sharp. It was bitter. It was disgusting.

That's when I knew that I had not pounced on Fudge at all. I had pounced on a skunk!

CHAPTER SEVEN

TOMATO IS NOT A DOG FLAVOR

There is nothing worse than being skunked.

It is even worse than going to jail. Talk about a terrible week.

Now things were *really* a mess. It was late. It was dark. There were no lights on in the house. The Duffs had already gone to bed. I couldn't go inside smelling like a skunk. But where could I go?

I thought about going down to the salt marsh. I could take a bath and roll in the sand. But it was too dark to walk down to the marsh.

The next best thing would be to wait for morning. I could get up at dawn. I would run down to the beach and get rid of this smell before anyone got up. I decided to sleep in the garage.

Unfortunately, both cars were in the garage. The garage was also filled with lots of junk. There was no place for me to lie down.

Fortunately, Mr. Duff had left the window of his car rolled down. I decided to sleep on the front seat. What choice did I have?

I was tired. I slept very well. After all, I'd had a very difficult day. I slept so well that I didn't wake up at dawn. In fact, I didn't even wake up when Mrs. Duff started cooking breakfast. I didn't wake up until Mr. Duff came out to the garage to get his car.

Now, I must tell you about Mr. Duff. He's big, and round, and he wears glasses. He also doesn't have much fur on the top of his head. I guess humans call that being bald.

Anyway, Mr. Duff is a very nice man. But he's grouchy. He yells sometimes. But I think he's grouchy from work. He calls me a fathead for no reason. And I never do anything to annoy anyone! All I ever do is rescue them!

Well, what happened next was an example of Mr. Duff's grouchiness problem. He came out to the garage and found me asleep on the front seat. He got very upset for no reason at all!

True, I didn't smell very good. But I didn't smell as bad as he seemed to think I did!

"Arnie, Katie, Martha!" he howled. "Get out here this instant! This fatheaded dog has done it again!"

Done what, I ask you? I have never been skunked in my life. What did he mean, again?

Well, they all came running out to the garage. Then they all started yelling, and holding their noses. Then Mrs. Duff ran inside. She came back out with a large can of tomato juice.

Mr. Duff was stomping and yelling about how he didn't have time to take the car in to Bob's Super-Special Car Wash. He also yelled about not having the money to pay for deskunking a car. But that was the least of my problems.

Before I could explain what happened, Mrs. Duff had poured the whole can of tomato juice all over me.

Now, I understand why she did this. I once read an article in *Field and Stream* about skunk smell and tomato juice. It seems that tomatoes have a special chemical in them that wipes out skunk smell. What they didn't tell you was that there is another way to get rid of skunk smell.

Going to the salt marsh, getting wet in salt water, and then rolling in sand mixed with seaweed also works very well. As a matter of fact, it gets rid of all kinds of dirt. There is only one small problem. Sometimes there's a dead fish in the seaweed. Sometimes you end up smelling like a dead fish. But that is not so bad. Skunk is definitely worse than dead fish.

Anyway, there I was on the morning of the Duff Pet Show, covered with tomato juice!

I was all red and matted and sticky. I stood

around waiting for someone to give me a bath. I stood around and stood around. But Mrs. Duff went into the house. Mr. Duff went off in the car. Katie went over to her boyfriend's house.

"Hey, Ma," Arnie finally said. "What about Fred? Are we going to have time to give him a bath before the pet show?"

"Oh, no," said Mrs. Duff from the porch. "We have to leave the tomato juice on him for several hours. That way, we'll make sure all the skunk smell is completely gone."

Several hours? But what about the pet show? What about my prize? What about my blue ribbon for Best in Show?

But no one seemed to care. So Arnie went to set up the ladder in the front yard. He wanted to hang the banner. No one said anything to me!

Except for that miserable Fudge, of course.

I was lying in the garage, minding my own business, when that troublemaker came in.

"Hey, Mom," he said. "What happened to you?"

"Nothing," I said.

"It smells like you got skunked," said Fudge. "How come you didn't know there was a skunk outside last night?"

I glared at him.

"We all knew about it," he said. "You can smell skunks even when they don't squirt— if you're a cat, that is."

Sometimes I really hate that cat. But then he came over and said, "Don't worry, Mom. I love you anyway."

That's when he gave me a lick. I hate that even worse. Getting kissed by a cat is disgusting!

"Wow!" said Fudge. "You taste great! What is that red stuff?"

I snarled at Fudge and told him to get lost. I was not in the mood for any of his crazy ideas.

The Duff Pet Show was supposed to start at two o'clock. At one o'clock, Katie came back with her boyfriend, Pete. She took one look at me and ran inside.

"Mom!" she yelled. "We can't have Fred at the pet show looking like that!"

"You're right," said Mrs. Duff. "I guess we'll just have to lock him in the garage until it's over."

And that's exactly what they did.

CHAPTER EIGHT

THE WORLD'S LOUDEST PET SHOW

Of course, without me, the Duff Pet Show was a disaster. I could have told them that. But do they ever see how much they need me? No. Not until the last minute.

There I was, locked in the garage. There they all were on the front lawn with four thousand pets. Well, maybe not four thousand. Maybe only twenty. But twenty pets are enough for a disaster.

All the children in the neighborhood came to the pet show. Each one brought a silly pet. There were dogs, cats, mice, gerbils, rabbits, and birds. You name it. They were all over the front lawn.

Of course, everyone knows what happens

when dogs meet cats. And you know what happens when cats see mice.

There was snarling. There was screeching. There was barking. There was yelling. I heard crashes, and groans. It was clear that the Duff Pet Show was in deep trouble. I stood up and looked out of the garage window.

I could just see the edges of the lawn. I saw a big black dog chase a little yellow cat down the side of the house. Both of them were being chased by children. I happen to know the dog. His name is King. He loves chasing cats. He loves that even more than chasing cars.

I saw a brown rabbit hop into a bush. I saw a little girl in a yellow sundress hop right after it.

I saw a small boy sitting against a tree. He was holding a carrot. I know that boy. His name is Charles. Charles never comes over to play with Arnie. Not that he's not a nice boy. It's just that Charles is allergic to everything furry. He is even allergic to me!

At first I thought that Charles was holding the carrot because he was planning to eat it. Then I remembered hearing something about a pet carrot. I guess the carrot was the only pet Charles could have.

Charles was sneezing and wheezing. It was a mistake for him to come to the pet show. He might not be allergic to carrots, but he sure was allergic to everything else there.

I saw a girl in a green pair of shorts put a mouse cage down on the lawn. Then the girl turned her back. A big, fluffy white cat crawled across the lawn on its belly. The cat moved right up to the mouse cage. He stuck a paw inside. The mice squeaked. The girl screamed. She grabbed her cage and started yelling at another little girl.

It was the loudest pet show I had ever heard.

It was clear that they needed my help. You cannot have cats, dogs, parrots, mice, lizards, bunnies, gerbils, snakes, and a carrot all on one lawn without me. They were going to need me soon.

It was time to break out of the garage. I used my old "shove on the back window" trick. First, I pushed a few cartons up against the window. Then I climbed on the cartons. I shoved the latch with my paw. It is one of those windows that has two hinges on the top. It is held shut by an old, rusty latch. Fortunately, Mr. Duff never remembers to fix the latch. I was out in no time.

I decided to take it slowly at first. After all, I didn't want to get locked up again. My plan was to stay out of sight until I was needed. I found a good bush and crawled underneath.

By this time, all the children had gotten their animals under control. Sort of. One tall poodle named Agatha was bouncing around on the end of her leash. But she has a nervous problem. She always does that. No one paid any attention.

They had already started the judging. Charles and his pet carrot were first. I suppose they did that so he could go home before he sneezed his brains out.

Charles's carrot won this prize: Crunchiest Pet. Now, is that ridiculous, or what?

That's when I saw, to my horror, that some crazy child had a tarantula for a pet. I have never trusted that little boy. His name is also Fred. I had, up until this moment, wanted to like him. After all, he had a great name. But he never seemed to act normal. Now I knew why!

When Fred came up to the judging table, he was holding a small glass cage. It looked like a little fish tank. Inside was this horrible thing! It was the fattest spider I have ever seen. It was big! It was furry! It had little pink toes! Yecch! It looked like something Beth would have around the house. But even Beth would not have liked *this* tarantula.

At that moment, I decided I had enough.

I jumped out from behind the bush. I wanted everyone to go home. Right now!

I started barking. I raced up to each pet and told them to go back to wherever they came from. They all did their best.

The dogs jerked loose from their leashes.

They ran behind the house. The cats all went up the oak tree. Everything else tried to get out of its cage or its jar or its tank. I was pleased. I knew that at any second, this silly pet show would be over and I could get some rest.

But I was wrong.

CHAPTER NINE

A MINOR RESCUE

"Fred!" yelled Katie. "You cut that out this very minute!"

I decided to ignore her. Here is what I have learned during my years as a rescue dog: Sometimes it pays to be deaf. I just pretend I don't understand English. After all, I am a dog, right? Dogs aren't supposed to understand English.

But not listening to Katie didn't help. Arnie came up and grabbed me. He held on to me while everyone collected their pets. This took some time. The cats who were up the tree were very difficult to get down.

They were about to start the judging again when suddenly Barney Brown ran up.

"Q-Tip is missing!" he yelled.

Q-Tip? What kind of a name is Q-Tip? I wondered. It sounds like something you use to clean your ears.

Well, it turned out that Q-Tip was a rabbit. A white rabbit, to be exact. I guess they named him Q-Tip because they thought he looked like a cotton ball or something. Well, I have seen a Q-Tip, and personally, I disagreed. Where was that little stick? Sometimes I wonder about humans.

"Now look what you've done!" yelled Katie. "Because of you and your silly barking, Barney's bunny is totally lost!"

Even Beth looked sort of upset. Arnie didn't look too happy either.

"Now you've ruined the entire pet show," yelled Katie. "Dad is right. You *are* a fathead!"

Normally I don't like being called a fathead. But when Katie calls me names, I don't mind. You see, she's a teenager. I read an article in *Seventeen* magazine about teenagers. It said they are moody, and often difficult.

In Katie's case, this is definitely true. Bad-tempered is more like it, I would say. But I don't mind. I just put up with her bad moods. I know that sooner or later, she'll get over them. Then she will be perfectly normal like everyone else.

Suddenly everyone started scurrying around. Before the judging could go on, Barney's bunny had to be found. Of course, they were going about it all wrong. For one thing, humans can't smell. All they can do is see and hear. Most of them are not very good at that, either. A dog can smell anything. We can tell things with our noses that humans don't even think about.

For example, we can smell the sidewalk and tell these things: who came up the walk; when; what they had for lunch before they came over; what kind of mood they are in. Humans can't tell a thing from smelling a sidewalk.

I knew that if I could get Arnie to let go of me, I could find Barney Brown's bunny. But Arnie was holding on very tight. That left me with only one way to handle the problem. I just had to drag Arnie around with me as I sniffed and looked. That is what I did.

I got the scent near the big oak tree. Then I followed it. I dragged Arnie through the bushes on the side of the house. I dragged Arnie up the porch. I dragged Arnie into the garbage can shed, through the garage, and back to the house. Then we went into the kitchen, into the hall closet, behind the couch, up the stairs, under all the beds, and finally into Katie's room. That rabbit had really run all over the place.

I followed my nose right up to Katie's bureau. The bottom drawer was open. I looked inside. Her sweaters were all messed up. She should really clean out her drawers. The rabbit scent was very strong in the sweaters. I stuck my nose in, and tossed a bunch of sweaters out of the way.

And guess what! There was Barney Brown's bunny.

Arnie grabbed the bunny before it could

run someplace else. I, Fred the Fearless, Protector of the Innocent, the Great Houdini of Dogs, had saved the day again.

But was anyone grateful? Well, Barney Brown was grateful. And Arnie was pleased, too. But Katie was very upset for some reason.

She said the whole thing was my fault in the first place. But she was wrong. After all, nobody else's pet got lost. Clearly Barney Brown was not taking proper care of his bunny. In addition, if it hadn't been for me, that bunny might have stayed lost forever. He might have gotten bored in Katie's sweaters. Who wouldn't? He could have run down to Main Street! He might have gotten hit by a car! It is lucky for everyone that I was there to save that bunny!

Katie, of course, had a lot of loud and not very nice things to say about me. This is because the bunny left bunny droppings all over her sweaters. But was this my fault? Of course not! Any normal person would be able to see this. It was the bunny's fault!

61

And then she started yelling about how there was tomato juice all over her sweaters, too.

But this wasn't my fault either. After all, it wasn't my idea to pour tomato juice all over myself and then not give me a bath.

You see what I mean about Katie? Sometimes she is very bad-tempered. And for no reason at all.

Finally we were able to calm everyone down, including Katie. We went back to judging the pet show.

CHAPTER TEN

THE DUMBEST PRIZE OF ALL

Well, they finally gave out all the prizes. Personally, I thought they were stupid prizes. There was Best Nose. That was given to Fritz the dachshund. That's the kind of dog some people call a hotdog dog. There was Silkiest Ears, won by Paloma, who is an Afghan hound. There was Shaggiest Fur, which was given to Bozo. I should tell you that Bozo is a mutt. I do not think his fur is shaggy. I think his fur is ratty. He looks like a moth-eaten couch, as far as I'm concerned. But I suppose they were trying to be nice.

There was Loudest Bark, won by this wirehaired terrier named MacDougal. That was also a mistake. I, Fred, have the loudest bark.

MacDougal has a very painful bark. His bark could shatter windows. They gave Fattest Tail to a white Persian cat, and Bluest Eyes to a Siamese kitten. Slimiest Skin went to Mary Lou, who is Beth's pet frog. I agreed with that prize. Mary Lou is definitely slimy. And, of course, Crunchiest Pet went to Charles's pet carrot. The tarantula won Most Legs. That was a good prize, too. Except I might have also given the tarantula Most Disgusting.

Best Hairdo went to Buster's guinea pig, and Thinnest Tail went to Walter's lizard. The snake won Best Slitherer, which I suppose is fair.

The prize they gave me, Fred Duff, was the dumbest prize of all. And it was all Fudge's fault.

Once things got going at the Pet Show again, Fudge came over and sat with Arnie and me. All he did was lick me. Every time he licked me, I swatted him with my paw. But each time, he just kept coming back to lick me again. Soon everyone was laughing.

Well, *they* might have thought it was pretty funny. But I didn't think so at all.

"Get lost, you little troublemaker," I kept saying.

He kept saying, "I love you, Mom."

"Buzz off, or I won't teach you how to read anymore," I threatened.

"I don't mind," said Fudge. "I already know how to read."

"I won't let you eat out of my food bowl anymore," I said.

"You don't let me eat out of your food bowl now," answered Fudge.

That cat is a pain in the neck.

What could I do? I mean, besides yanking his tail, or nipping his ear. But I would never do that. I am against violence of any kind. Even violence to cats. You can see how kindhearted and peaceful I am. Many dogs do not feel that way about cats. But I am a very noble dog.

"What is your problem, Fudge?" I said. I was getting very annoyed.

"You taste terrific," said Fudge. His eyes

were half-closed. "What is all over your fur?"

"It's tomato juice, you idiot," I answered. "Cats do not like tomato juice!"

"You are wrong," said Fudge. "I love tomato juice and I am a cat."

He kept right on licking me. That is why I won the prize I did. It was not Best in Show. It was not Most Noble Dog. It was not Best Rescuer on the Planet.

Thank goodness the *Big Bluff News* forgot to send the reporters. The prize I got was Best-Tasting Pet.

I ate the ribbon when they gave it to me. There is no way I want that thing lying around the house for everyone to see.

Well, despite all the disasters and all the mess, the Duff Pet Show was finally over. All the pets went home. The yard got cleaned up. And I was finally given a bath.

Soon we were all sitting around in the living room. Mr. and Mrs. Duff seemed pleased with the day.

BEST TASTING PET

"I thought it was wonderful that each child won a prize," said Mrs. Duff.

"And I think it was wonderful that nobody's pet got eaten," said Mr. Duff. That was his idea of a joke.

"I think it was wonderful that Fred found Barney's bunny," said Arnie. At least someone sticks up for me around here.

"I think it's wonderful that all my sweaters got ruined," said Katie, making a grouchy face.

"I think you're wonderful, Mom," said Fudge. "You can lick me anytime you want."

I didn't answer. I would rather lick the inside of a gas can.

I tried to go to sleep. It had been a hard week. I had been arrested. I had been sent to jail. I had been skunked. I had been licked by a cat. I had been laughed at. I had not won Best in Show. But at least it was over.

I was sure that I would never have a terrible week like this one again. After all, what else could possibly happen?

You should only know!

The End